E Schwanda
Schwanda, JC.
Sprinkles' first haircut

P v

# Sprinkles' First Haircut

by JC Schwanda    illustrated by Dan Kanemoto

Simon Spotlight/Nick Jr.
New York   London   Toronto   Sydney

Based on the TV series *Blue's Clues*® created by Traci Paige Johnson,
Todd Kessler, and Angela C. Santomero as seen on Nick Jr.®

 SIMON SPOTLIGHT
An imprint of Simon & Schuster Children's Publishing Division
1230 Avenue of the Americas, New York, New York 10020
© 2008 Viacom International Inc. All rights reserved. NICK JR., *Blue's Clues*, *Blue's Room*, and all
related titles, logos, and characters are trademarks of Viacom International Inc.
Created by Traci Paige Johnson, Todd Kessler, and Angela C. Santomero. All rights reserved,
including the right of reproduction in whole or in part in any form.
SIMON SPOTLIGHT and colophon are registered trademarks of Simon & Schuster, Inc.
Manufactured in the United States of America
First Edition 10 9 8 7 6 5 4 3 2 1
ISBN-13: 978-1-4169-5442-2
ISBN-10: 1-4169-5442-2

Blue and her little brother, Sprinkles, were sitting down to read a great book. Something was not quite right.

"Blue," said Sprinkles, "I can't see the book very well."

"Uh-oh!" said Blue. "I think I know why." Blue noticed something looked different about Sprinkles.

"Your hair is so long," Blue said, "it's covering your eyes!"

"It is?" Sprinkles said.

"Do you know what that means?" asked Blue with a smile.

"What?" asked Sprinkles in a quiet voice.

"It's time for your first haircut!" Blue cheered.

Roar E. Saurus heard the news and
rushed in.

"Rooooar!" he roared. "A first haircut?
What an exciting day!"

Sprinkles didn't look very excited.

"What's wrong, Sprinkles?" asked Frederica. "You're going to look great with your new haircut."

"I'm a little scared," Sprinkles said. "I've never had my hair cut before."

Big sister Blue knew just what to do. "We have to show Sprinkles there's nothing to worry about when going to the barbershop!"

"What's the barbershop?" asked Sprinkles.

Blue asked Silly Seat and Dress-Up Chest to help them show
Sprinkles what a barbershop looked like.

"First you sit in a big, comfy seat," said Frederica.

"Then you have a cape wrapped around you like this," said Blue.

"Look at me, I'm Barber Roar E.," said Roar E. Saurus, pretending.

"There's nothing scary about him—right, Sprinkles?" Blue pointed out.

"Nope," Sprinkles answered.

*Doodl-ee, doodl-ee, doodl-ee, doodl-ee, Doodle Board!*

"Doodle Board has a doodle-doodle guessing game for us to play," said Blue.

"He's doodling what tools a barber uses," Roar E. said.

*Doodle, doodle, doodle, guess!*

"I wonder what those are." Frederica scratched her head.

"It's a comb and scissors!" shouted Sprinkles.

"You got it!" cheered Blue.

Sprinkles got very quiet. "What if the scissors hurt?" he whispered.

"They won't," said Blue. "I'd never let anything hurt my little brother.

"Okay, it's time to go to the real barbershop," Blue said. "We'll get there by jumping into this picture. Ready, Sprinkles?"

"I'm ready," he said.

"Wow, look at how cool the barbershop is," said Blue.

A man came over and shook Sprinkles' paw. He was wearing the same shirt Roar E. was!

"Hi there, Blue! Welcome, Sprinkles. I'm Barber Bob."

"Barber Bob, my little brother, Sprinkles, is just a little nervous," explained Blue. "Will cutting his hair hurt?"

"Not one bit," Barber Bob answered. "I promise."

Sprinkles smiled . . . just a little.

"But first," Barber Bob announced, "we have to shampoo your hair. Do you know what that means, Blue?"

"Yep," answered Blue. "We need a shampoo song!"

And so they sang.

*Rub Rub Rub*
*Scrub Scrub Scrub*
*See those bubbles* POP POP POP
*Rub Rub Rub*
*Scrub Scrub Scrub*
*Now you're clean way up top!*

Bubbles popped and Sprinkles giggled.

"Let's sing it again," he cheered.

BILLINGS COUNTY PUBLIC SCHOOL
Box 307
Medora, North Dakota 58645

"What do you think Barber Bob will dry your hair with?" asked Blu

"A big, fluffy towel?" Sprinkles guessed.

"You're getting good at this," said Barber Bob.

Sprinkles looked at himself in the mirror. He looked very silly. He was happy, and not the least bit nervous.

"Okay, Sprinkles, are you ready for your first haircut?" asked Barber Bob.

"Yes, I am," said Sprinkles.

"And you're not worried?" asked Blue.

"No, I am not," said Sprinkles.

Barber Bob moved the scissors up to Sprinkles' hair. . . .

"Wait. Stop!" said Blue. "Sprinkles, you never told us *how* you want your hair cut."

"How?" asked Sprinkles.

"Oh, you are right, Blue," said Barber Bob. "There are all kinds of styles. Do you want your hair short or long? Straight or curly?"

Sprinkles imagined all of his choices. Which one would look best?

After some thinking, Sprinkles announced, "I know which one I want."
Which one would it be?

"I think you chose the perfect hairdo," said Blue. "You look just like . . . yourself."

Everyone congratulated Sprinkles on his very first haircut.

"Thank you!" Sprinkles said. "You showed me there was nothing to be scared of."

"You're welcome," said Blue. "Now, let's go read that book!"